CW01370951

Bedsit Bohemia

A Sort of Romance

By

Jacob Louis Beaney

Bedsit Bohemia
by
Jacob Louis Beaney

Published by Hickathrift Press
ISBN 978 0 9954810 1 5
© Jacob Louis Beaney 2017

www.hickathriftpress.co.uk

Prologue

NONE OF this takes place in a bedsit. I came up with the title for the book before I wrote it and you know it's really hard to come up with a good title so I decided to keep it despite its utter irrelevance. 'Bedsit Bohemia' sounded like the sort of thing that I thought I was going to be or should be writing about. In my mind I was going to live in a tiny bedsit garret and live the life of a vagabond bohemian artiste...drinking red wine for breakfast, eating hard boiled quails eggs from the buttocks of a midget and never washing my pants.
I thought that's what artists were supposed to do.
But unfortunately this book isn't about any of that because none of that stuff happened to me.
  In actuality I ended up going in the complete opposite direction and moved to a leafy bourgeoisie suburb. The air filled with the deafening sound of middle-class children being forced to practice the cello and the streets pronged with swathes of passive aggressive middle aged couples arguing about Volvo's and catchment areas.
  So without the cliched romantic tropes of the bohemian artist to fall back on what was I going to write about?
  I began to think of the things that make a good book: Adventure, Travel, Tragedy and Romance I thought. A bit of sex and drugs and a sprinkling of bondage and boy wizards. Unfortunately this book has none of that in it either. So no bedsits and no wizards.
  So if you have picked this up in hope of getting some hot bedsit action then you are going to be thoroughly disappointed.
In fact you're probably going to be disappointed anyway. I have to confess that one of the main reasons for even attempting to write anything in the first place is that I have loads of ISBN numbers

that I have to use up before they expire. They cost me a lot of money and I don't want to waste them. For those that don't know an ISBN is like a registration number for a book, it's on the back cover above the barcode. It basically means you can sell it in book shops and things like that.

I'd written a book previously to this one but unfortunately they don't sell them singley and now I'm stuck with loads of them. I have to write 5 books over the next few years and without any ideas or noteworthy experiences I have no idea what I'm going to write them about.

So this book ended up being an attempt to include all the things that would normally make a good book. To be honest the rest is a desperate effort to scrabble together enough material to meet the minimum word requirement.

Generally it is agreed that a book has plot, characters and narrative.
Which unfortunately this doesn't have either
But at its very basics a book has to have words.
But no one has said what these words have to say or mean. They don't even have to be particularly good words. I'll save the complexities of character, plot and dialogue for those that have the time and inclination to indulge in such extravagances. I'll start basic. Some words.
All I knew was that I needed to write 10,000 words about something or other.
And I did.
And despite what you may think of the results, I've written a book and no one can take that away from me.
And if you have nothing positive to say about this book when you get to the end of it, you can't say there weren't at least words in it.
So there you have it. A book whose title bares no relation to its contents and was only written out of a fear of wasting money.
I hope you enjoy it.

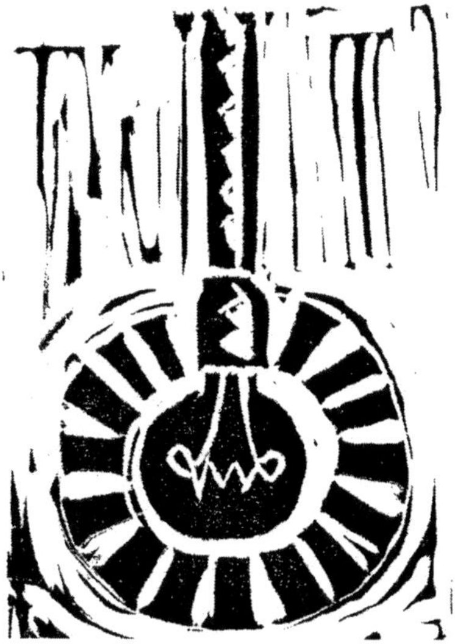

Book 1

Adventure

1

The Sofa

ONCE MORE I found myself occupying the sofa in my Nans old council house in the sunny seaside ghetto where I grew up. My Nan had been dead for a while now and my uncle now acted as unofficial guardian over our humble family estate. This estate consisting of a 3 bedroom council house, an allotment and a wheelbarrow. Of course no one wanted him to be as he was by all accounts a thieving, lying, crazy, junky bastard. But he had hidden the will and there was nothing much we could do about it apart from wait patiently for him to overdose or be sent back to prison for some crime he had no doubt committed.

I was at the end of a cycle I had been trapped in since I reached adulthood. I would move to some strange city, involve myself in a self-destructive love affair with someone clearly unhinged and then have it all predictably turn to shit. I'd soon find myself back home on this very sofa where I'd spend the next few months depressed and wondering why everything had gone so horribly wrong. Then I'd pick myself up, dust myself off and having learnt nothing start the whole cycle off again.

I'd just been returning from a stretch in Hull where I had an unfortunate romance with a women whose only thing we had in common is that we were both psoriasis sufferers. We'd met at a speed dating evening and just as our date was heading for disaster I noticed a small patch of inflamed glimmering hope on her left knuckle, which I knew at once to be psoriasis.

It became an immediate talking point. We ended up going back to hers, exploring every inch of each others pustular inflamed bodies. We made love all night, our bodies rubbing against each other causing our skin lesions to rub off like coastal erosion creating a mountain of flakey dead white skin cells to form around the bed.

We dated for a while but eventually she broke up with me when her psoriasis was cured by a Chinese herbal medicine specialist and we had nothing left to talk about.

Since adulthood I had found myself drifting from one place to another and had developed the habit of publishing my observations and life experiences in a series of books. These had started to develop a readership amongst mainly middle aged male, alcoholic perverts and woman with acute mental health conditions and sciatica.

My dream ever since I was a little child had been to develop a debilitating drug addiction and live in a squalid, damp bedsit spending all day drinking cheap wine and writing poetry on a battered type writer. But it was proving harder than imagined to achieve. For one thing it was really hard to find printing ribbon and drugs seemed to cost an absolute fortune.

2

The City

IT WAS while I was back home that my paths crossed with my estranged cousin who was similarly down on his luck. We'd been the best of friends in childhood but had fallen out at our Granddads funeral when my then girlfriend had given him a consolatory handjob in the disabled toilets at the crematorium.

"He just seemed so sad..." had been her reasoning.

He was currently in the middle of a bitter divorce and suggested we get a place together in N, which was a city close to where we grew up which was often described as "Nice".

It was a very ancient city and so full of oldness that you couldn't throw a stone without hitting a monument, a castle or a site where a load of Victorian prostitutes had been horrifically murdered. It was a shame that the rest of the city followed the same homogeneous blue print that all English cities seem to have...there being the really old bit, the posh bit, the council estate bit and the bit that's in the process of gentrification which is simultaneously posh and scummy where you can buy either heroin or a loaf of artisanal sour dough bread depending on what day it was. And of course there was the shopping mall, two in fact, a Gregg's bakery and a ghostly empty branch of Woolworths which was waiting patiently to become a Pound Shop.

There had been a long and bitter historical rivalry between between N and our home town of Yarpool. Normally we wouldn't have considered the move but as the entirety of the UK outside of London was now one endless poverty stricken cesspit it **hardly** seemed to matter where you lived. Of course my old man wouldn't approve of me living in N. Betraying my roots he'd no doubt call it. But he said that one time when he caught me eating hummus.

The main source of industry and income for Yarpool had been the potato mines, where deep underground ancient potatoes lurked the size of a Ford Fiesta. Some said these had been slowly growing since the time of the dinosaurs and others said that this probably wasn't true. My Dad, Grandad and Great Grandad had all worked these pits before their closure by Thatcher in the 80's. And of course there was also the seal industry. But the fleeting delicacy of seal steak and seal fur handbags had long since drifted out of vogue. As a result of the demise of these noble industries the majority of Yarpool was now unemployed and skint and as a result the citizens of N looked down on us considering us philistinic, incestuous, inbred bumpkins. They had a fancy theatre, an arts centre and an opera house where as our main cultural pastime was to drink 3 litres of cheap cider and to see how far you could skid a slice of ham across the marshes*.

Our new house was situated in a area named by estate agents as 'The Golden Square' which was a leafy, middle-class suburb mainly populated by twats. Around the city there was also the Silver Triangle, the Bronze Rectangle and at the lower end of the housing spectrum the less desirable Lead Octagon and Pewter Rhomboid.

In the middle of these metallic geometrically named housing areas was a large central park nicknamed Hypodermic Park where all the cities junkies would go to shoot up topless in the summer. It was full of vicious shitting illegal dogs, needles and drug dealers but despite all this was still rather pleasant

---

*My own record being a respectable 12. The town record for this is 38 where by it reached the neighbouring town of Cornby, which being even more deprived was swiftly eaten by it's inhabitants. Mud covered Sliced Ham being regarded there as the finest of delicacies.

My cousin spent the majority of his time in our new house drinking whiskey whilst weeping uncontrollably at the dining room table. It got so bad that his tears began to erode the varnish off the table to the extent that we lost some money from our damages deposit.

One of the main advantages of living with him, despite being kept up all night by his heart wrenching sobbing, was that he was head barrister at a coffee house in the city and as a result would often bring home litres and litres of ever so slightly gone off milk.

3

Le Plonguer

I WORKED on a zero hours contract as a dishwasher at a local Organic Gluten Free Vegan Macrobiotic Restaurant. Well I say dishwasher. As part of the restaurants low carbon, sustainability ethos all the plates, cups, bowls, cutlery and utensils were made from an edible type of corn, with the idea being that the customer would eat them as well as their meal saving the environment by not using all that hot water and washing up liquid. Unfortunately these never got eaten as they tasted like a urinary tract infection.

It was my duty as 'dishwasher' to finish off any left over crockery. When I was mid way through a shift and had hit a edible corn plate wall the restaurant manager would come up behind me:

"There are children starving in Africa..." he would say patting me on the back encouragingly "Those kids would give their right arm to stand here night after night eating this delicious and nutritious corn based bounty... And to think I'm even paying you for the privilege! You should think your self lucky"

At the end of a shift I was bloated and nauseated having gotten through several half dozen half eaten bowls, plates, knifes, forks and serving ladles. In the end I tried to get out of this duty by crumbling up the bowls into a secret compartment in my trousers which operated by a leaver I would eject into the parking lot when I took a cigarette break.

On one occasion I ate an entire set of ramekins, only to discover that they were the only thing in kitchen that wasn't made from corn.

The job was diabolical. And as it was on a zero hours contract meant I was finacially insecure and constantly broke. Though it gave me the privilege to observe and overhear the clientele, a class of people I had so far been unfamiliar with:

"On the menu here, what is this?"
"It's a herbaceous annual plant grown as a grain crop primarily for its edible seeds"
"Hm"
"Poor brown people eat it in 3rd world countries"
"Oh really? I'll have it"

"How's John?"
"I've stuck him in a travelodge"
"What on earth happened?"
"I left him in charge of the Waitrose delivery the other day and he goes and orders the squeezy bottle of mayonnaise. I mean after 25 years you'd have thought he would have had more sense. And me with my diploma in interior décor, imagine if the girls would have seen something so ascetically vulgar like that in my kitchen? I would never have lived it down. I said "John, I'm beginning to think our whole marriage is a sham" and I sent him packing..."
"What a bastard"

"So I said to them: "I appreciate that this is a compulsory vegetarian Hare Krishna commune, but I've got some rose water harissa paste, a bottle of good merlot and I'm cooking this fucking chicken"

4

Bad Drunk

I'D STARTED drinking heavily to block out the reality that I was 32 and my only source of income depended on me eating vast quantities of edible corn crockery. In one particularly booze sodden week I managed to consumed 106 ½ pints of cheap lager, 6 double whiskeys, 3 litres of cider, a double baileys, a ¾ bottle of Advocaat that had been in the cupboard since Christmas and a strange liquid a homeless man had offered me out of his shoe. At the end of this week my skin had turned bright yellow and I had to spend a few days on the sofa with a bag of frozen peas on my liver.

I'm an notoriously bad drunk and these nights of heavy drinking would often find me most mornings waking in a cocktail of my own bodily fluids. The sheets a visceral rainbow of blood, piss and sperm. Upon opening my eyes I would be tormented by early morning cringe-inducing flashbacks of the night before...vague blurry recollections of vomiting into the neighbours recycling bin, urinating onto a sleeping hedgehog and stealing a slice of pizza from a man in a wheelchair.

I have four brothers who are also bad drunks and we no doubt inherit this from our father who got it from his father who got it from his father and so on until the very first fish that crawled out of the ocean, who if he had the capacity, a basic knowledge of chemistry and some rudimentary equipment for home brewing would of no doubt have also been a bad drunk.

When we were kids, every Wednesday the old man would cash the family allowance and go straight to the pub with it. He would turn up in the early hours of the morning, bleary eyed and shouting incomprehensible gibberish about the 80's and Thatcher and then proceed to smash all phones in the house in case "The Government were listening".

We would often have to tie him up with our school ties and bundle him into the cupboard under the stairs until he calmed down a bit. This became such a regular occurrence that still to this day I'll inadvertently refer to the cupboard under the stairs as the 'Drunk Tank'.

Once I'd gotten so drunk I think I may have gotten off with an elderly homeless women at a bus shelter. I woke up the next morning with sores around my lips and the taste of Frosty Jacks and stale cigarettes in my mouth. I got her number though, which was just directions to some bins behind Argos.

On another occasion I was so drunk I fell out of my bedroom window while trying to open it and now have no memories of the years 1996 – 2004.

5

Scurvy

ANOTHER ONE of the benefits of living with my cousin is that he was too depressed to cook so he often ordered take-aways which he was then too depressed to eat. These often ended up in the bin and when he was asleep inevitably they ended up inside me.

With a diet that mainly comprised of edible corn plates, alcohol and half eaten take away food from the bin I inevitably got sick.

"You have scurvy" the doctor told me

"And also despite being malnourished you're still quite overweight"

"I don't understand, is there anything I can do to get rid of this? Surgery? Aromatherapy? I'll try anything."

He raised above me a strange spherical object that was bright orange in colour. My mouth dropped open in awe.

"This is an O-R-A-N-G-E you need to eat more of these and other F-R-U-I-T-S"

*

"Would it kill you to throw away some fruit once in a while! You're killing me!" I shouted at my cousin when I got in.
He raised his head from his pool of tears and looked at me with a confused expression.

6

The Pizza and The Pretty Homeless Girl

IT ALWAYS made me a little depressed to see the disgusting imbalance of wealth on display in the city. How you could have a travel agent advertising luxury Caribbean holidays and huddled in the adjacent doorway would be an elderly homeless man, half mad and caked in his own excrement.

I was walking through the city one cold drizzly night my arms clutching a large warm pizza box. I was eager to find the first appropriate bench, alcove or nook to sit on and shovel its contents into my face.

I turned the corner and was approached by a pretty, young homeless girl. I was taken aback that despite her dirty clothes and filthy face by how fragile and angelic she looked.

    She explained that she'd become homeless and had lost her job as she was always so late and tired having been sleeping rough on the streets. She'd told me how one night while on the streets she'd been beaten up by a gang of drunk men who had broken her ribs. I said that I was sorry that I didn't have any money to help her as I worked on a zero hours contract eating corn crockery for a living. I offered her a slice of my pizza and taking a slice she thanked me, smiled and walked off back into the night.

    I sat down at the bus station and began to weep at how sad and fucked the world was while cramming a tear stained slice of pizza into my blubbering face.

7

Middle-Class, Metropolitan, Liberal Elite

ONE OF the main problems of living in an area mainly populated by the metropolitan, middle-class, liberal, elite is that they were always coming around your house with clipboards asking you to sign petitions or shoving flyers through your door.

These door-to-door campaigners all had skin the colour of A4 copier paper and appeared to visibly struggle with the weight of their clipboards.

"Sir, we are talking to people today about an issue that we think is of great significance to the future of democracy in this country. Will you sign this petition to guarantee political suffrage for cruciferous and root vegetables?"

"Er, no sorry I'm not interested"

"You mean you're not interested that the humble broccoli and noble parsnip be given a fair inclusion into the democratic process??" He left broken and disgusted his mind unable to comprehend why someone would have such apathy for something of such momentous importance.

8

Stubbs

OCCASIONALY AS an act of charity I would be invited to swarees given by wealthy patrons of the restaurant. I think they saw me as something of a novelty...

"I'm a dog psychiatrist" Announced the man standing beside me at the buffet table.
"Oh yeah?" I said trying with every ounce of my being to appear interested.
"I wrote my thesis on post-traumatic stress disorder in border collies"
"Actually…" I said, suddenly lightning up with a spark of mischief "My jack russell tried to kill himself last week by hanging himself on his own lead. He even left a suicide not in crumbled dog biscuits…"
"You'll have to bring him in, could be serious, jack russells are prone to depression, it all stems from fears of abandonment due to their large litter sizes"
"Oh sorry, I was joking…"
"Canine suicide is no laughing matter."
The sense of disapproval filled the air like a cloud of poisonous gas.
"So, what did you study?" said the dog psychiatrist reluctantly after a few minutes of uncomfortable silence.
"Art."
"Oh."

We both stood staring awkwardly at a large untouched dish of Kalamata olives.
"I saw a good show in London last week, some exquisite pieces by Stubbs" he volunteered after some considerable time. "That man definitely had an exceptional understanding of the equine form"
"Stubbs? Was he the guy that did all the old paintings of fat horses?"
"I better go find my wife"
I stood alone at the buffet table scanning the room filled with tree surgeons, sand therapists and one guy I met who was a house plant masseuse. Deep down I knew that all these people intrinsically hated me because I was the type of person who drank red wine out of a pint glass, got all his clothes from George Asda and dipped oven chips into hummus. God they look so good though, the women so glowing and radiant, I wonder if they use a special type of soap they don't tell poor people about.? It would be nice if one of them had sex with me, just once, as an act of charity, like giving 20p to a tramp...
I let out a deep sigh before filling my pockets full of smoked salmon canapés and a dripping wet block of feta. Shoving an oily handful of olives into my face I grabbed a bottle of red wine off the bar and walked home alone.
When I got in I poured myself a pint of wine, got into bed and googled who Stubbs was.
That man really knew how to paint a horse.

9

Book

ONCE I had settled into my place the serious business of the novel writing began. Armed with my trusty type writer all I needed now was some ink ribbon and some profound human truths to write about.

10

Sandwiches

I STOOD in Asda staring at the sandwiches in the reduced section. I thought it would be a good idea for a chapter.
But it wasn't.

11

The Human Condition

I STOOD staring meaningfully at the recycling bin. Were the little metal tins for bake well tarts recyclable or not?
I couldn't decide.
But I knew they said something profound about the human condition.
So I thought I better include it.

12

Wasps

"YOU DON'T want to buy those chocolate bars mate they've got wasps in them"
I revealed myself from my hidden position behind the stacks of bargain multi-pack toilet rolls.
"I'm sorry, but did I just over hear you saying that those chocolate bars have wasps in them?
"Yeah, what's it got to do with you?" he asked me suspiciously
"Oh nothing really, it's just I'm writing a book and I'm little short

of things to write about and that sounded quite interesting..."

"Oh yeah, what's the book about?"

"It's about a man who doesn't live in a bedsit and hasn't got any ideas to write a book about. This whole thing will probably be a chapter"

"Doesn't sound like it's going to be a very good book, you should try putting some boy wizards in there. Boy wizards and bondage that's what people like to read about, not overheard conversations about insects in chocolate bars in a Pound Land"

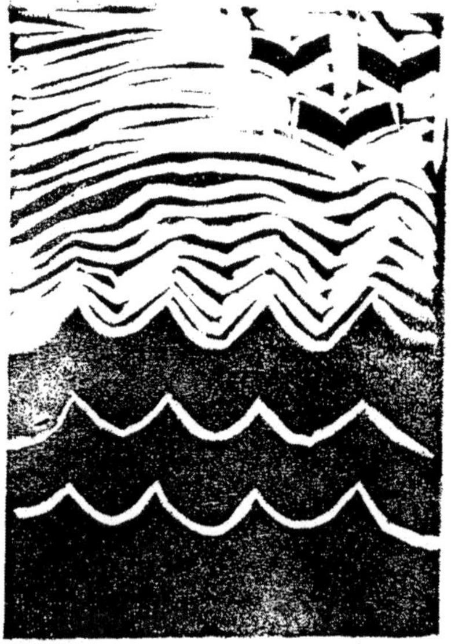

Book 2

Travel

13

Crab Sticks

I NEEDED to go somewhere exotic, somewhere far flung where I could have exiting adventures to write about. At the bus station I counted my change and asked the lady at the ticket office how far £3.50 would get me.

Claxon is a tiny seaside village about 45 minutes from N and at £3.50 return it was as exotic as I could get. All I knew about the place is that it was famous for its giant edible crabs.

I wondered the deserted coastal village in the drizzle taking in the sights of its boarded up arcades, closed fish and chip shops, empty caravans and burnt out graffiti covered chalets as the haunting melody of an ice cream truck roaming the desolate streets echoed in the distance.

I went to the park to feed the ducks but there weren't any. The only local wildlife in sight was a an overweight rat asleep in a puddle of it's own vomit and a one legged, one eyed seagull which was eating the contents of a used nappy.

I walked past a shop with a peeling hand painted sign of a crab above it only to realise that crabs were out of season.

I got some frozen crab sticks out of Iceland and waited at the bus shelter for them to defrost. Eating the partially thawed crab sticks I watched a pack of obese hoodies next to me who were smoking skunk and watching videos of a woman being sodomised by a horse on their mobile phones.

The sounds of the woman moaning, the horse neighing and the twinkle of the ice cream truck in the distance filled the dull wet streets as I waited patiently for the bus home.

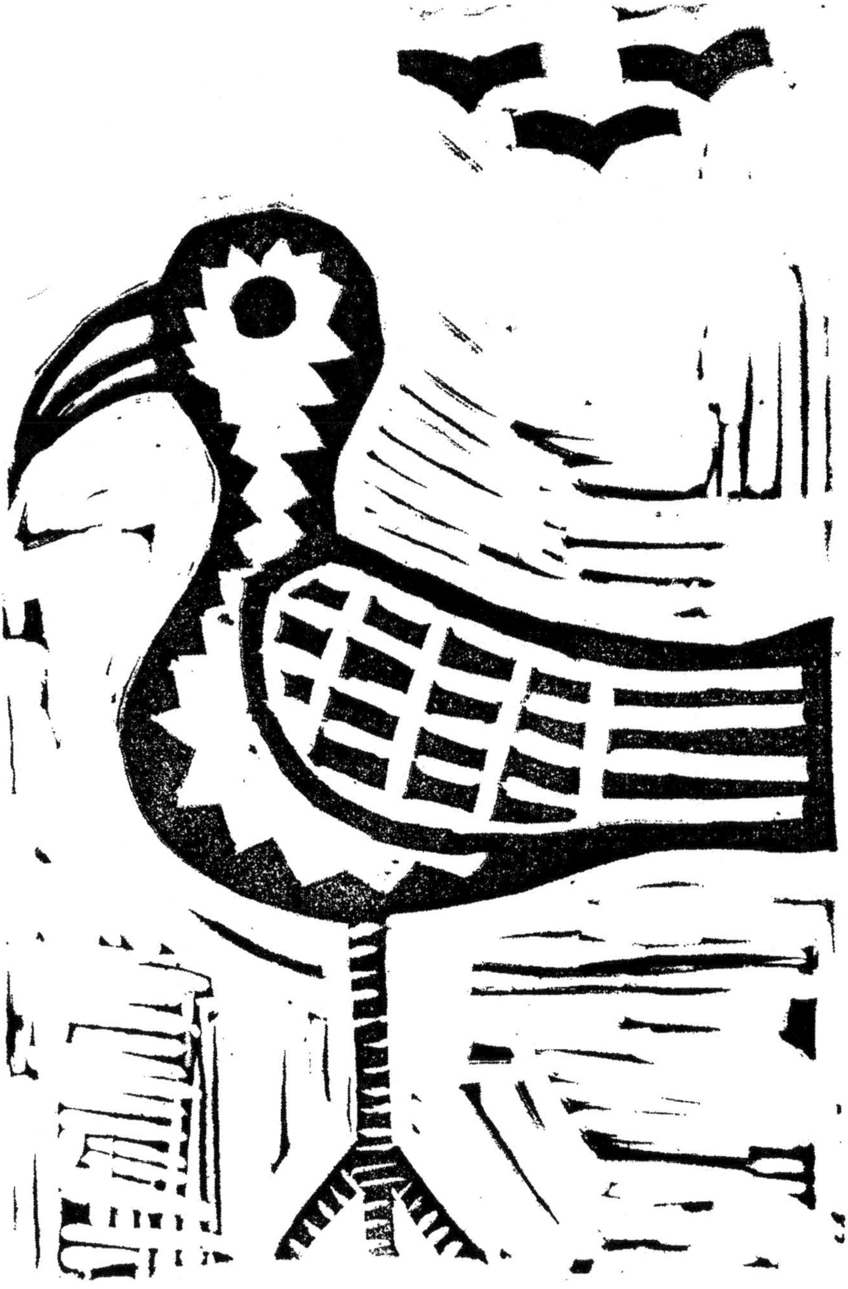

*This part of the book was going to be bigger but unfortunately I didn't have any money to go anywhere else.

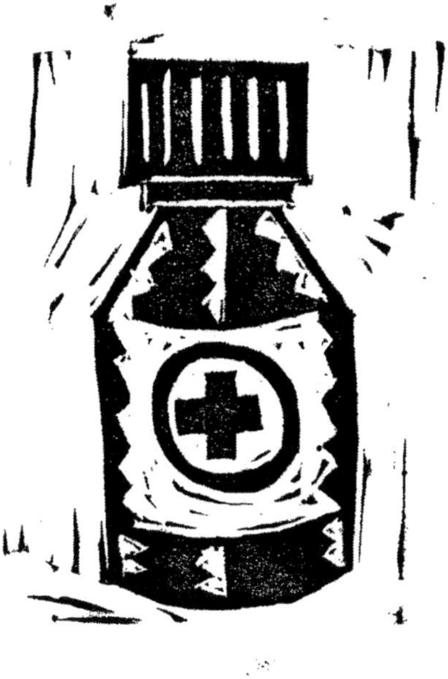

Book 3

Tragedy

14

Tragedy

TRAGEDY WAS always a good source for material. Some lucky people can get whole books out of a close relative dying, a self-destructive drug addiction, an interesting medical condition or even just having being molested by an uncle as a kid.

Unfortunately none of that stuff happened to me.

I'm slightly overweight and have haemorrhoids and when I was 12 I walked in on my uncle watching a video of an overweight German woman defecating onto a glass coffee table as a man lay naked underneath it...but I don't know what to classify that as. Looking at my current word count I'm going to need some pretty tragic things to start happening soon.

15

The Death Of Mullet Jean

AS LUCK would have it my Aunty called me unexpectedly to inform me that my Nan's old friend Mullet Jean had died a few days ago and that the funeral service was today. Within minutes I was dressed head to toe in black and on the bus to Yarpool. All I could really remember about Jean was that she had a mullet. That and her skin, it was bright orange and so wrinkled it looked like someone had drawn a face on a dried apricot.

How was I going to eek out a chapter on this I thought to myself on the bus.

It seems I wasn't the only one for whose Jeans hair style was the most prominent thing in their memory of her. Jeans Mullet was mentioned a total of 47 times in her brief eulogy.

I stared at the mini scotch eggs and pork pie segments on the buffet table.

I debated whether it would be wrong to steal the food from a dead old women you hardly knew and whose funeral you were only at to gain material for a book. I decided that if she was up in heaven looking down she would probably think it was OK. At least I guessed so anyway. Like I say I hardly knew her.

I looked over and saw my aunty discreetly jamming prawn vol-au-vents into her handbag.

I started filling my pockets with bacon quiche for the journey back.

16

The Death of Uncle David

He'd been dead for three days when they found him. Overdose.
Apparently the dogs had been at him.
They had to be put down as once they get a taste for human flesh...
Well, there's just no going back to pedigree chum for them

Having no money he was buried by the state.
They put the body in what looked like an enormous shoe box
And he was taken away in a transit van
The transit van was filthy and someone had drawn a smiley face in the dirt

He was taken to the incinerator out of town and placed on a large conveyor belt
with all the other unwanted, unloved things
The hundreds of unmarked shoe boxes slowly rumbled towards the inferno
As plumes of jet black smoke puffed rhythmically from the chimney.

He'd always spoken of what songs he wanted played at his funeral
But in the end all he got was what ever was playing on the radio in the transit van on the short drive to the incinerator
Something on Kiss FM no doubt.
Or some other shit.

17

Under the Spell of The Green Pixie

... I gazed around at my bare and squalid lodgings. The room was littered with empty measuring spoons, mucous encrusted tissues and what appeared to be Pringles tubes full of excrement the dirty contents inexplicably taped up with parcel tape.
A bare garish bulb illuminated my gaunt naked body on the filthy soiled mattress as I'd just remembered I'd sold the lampshade last week...

All the signs were there...
the excessive mucous, the measuring spoons, the blatant disregard for soft furnishings...I'd fallen under the spell of the Green Pixie and had developed a debilitating, destructive and life dependent addiction to Night Nurse, or as it's variously known on the streets as...Juice, Our Green Lady, The Emerald Wizard, The Viridian Matron etc.

...It had started a few weeks ago when I had a cold and went to the chemists...before I knew it I was hooked on its soothing sedative properties and was buying four bottles a day. The chemist soon became aware to my excessive consumption and alerted The Filth. My face was now plastered up in all the chemists in the city. Unable to score I had to travel to all the chemists in the county wearing a

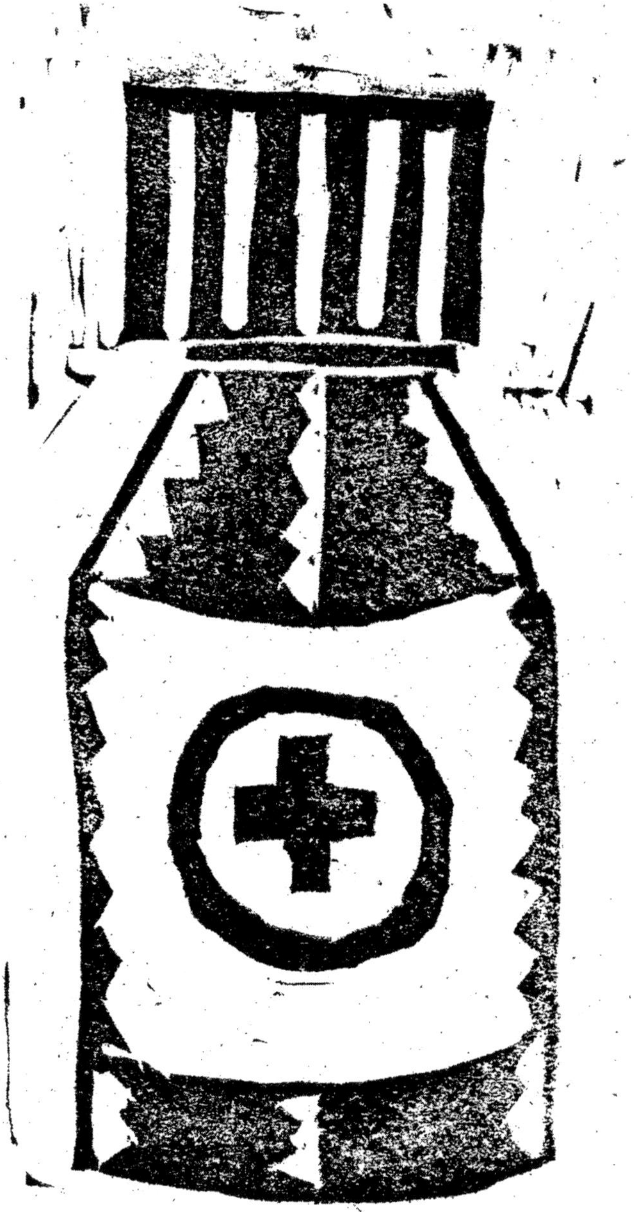

variety of wigs and beards I'd made from the hair I'd shaved off stray dogs.

...I looked around the room, rays of garish sunlight pierced my eyes as I'd just remember I'd sold the curtains a few days ago...You knew the addiction had you bad when you suddenly began to disregard the importance of interior décor.
So this was bohemia...the irony being that I couldn't even write about it as I sold all the vowels on my typewriter to the pawn shop.

To make matters worse I'd been suspended from work for 'inappropriate dress'. I'd sold my remaining pair of trousers and was sent home when I turned up for work in
a pair of shorts I'd made from stapled together Kebab shop flyers.

The Menthol Kid

...I was getting desperate...no dough and no means to score. The Menthol Kid told me to meet him at his place as he'd found a way to make his own green pixie. When I got there he had a large saucepan on the go...
"ere get your lips on some of this" he said with a toothless smile
It was a foul and potent concoction made from what turned out to be limeade, fairy washing up liquid and methadone...basically anything green he could get his hands on. It certainly gave you a buzz...but it just didn't have the same drowsy euphoria as Our Green Lady.

Daddy Day Nurse

Daddy Day Nurse had been on the green juice for the last two decades...such a long exposure to the stuff had resulted in severe arterial and neurological damage and as a result his body had degenerated into little more than a shrivelled head on a skateboard. He managed to move himself along with his tongue which was black and covered in gravel and cigarette butts.

It was a common sight amongst juice heads of that age...the only way they could score was to lap up any spilt medication on the floors in chemists...or by blowing dwarfs for 20 ml of an own brand cough medicine.

Daddy Day Nurse told us of a new government scheme where you could get clean.

The process involved being administered 3 black currant sore throat sweets a day as a rectal suppository over a period of 12 weeks...

...If he stuck out the whole 12 weeks they said they would put him forward for an operation to have his body rebuilt with a type of flesh coloured play dough...

With Daddy Day Nurse in tow we went down to the community hospital and signed our selves up...hoping that we would at last awake from this most dreadful spell...

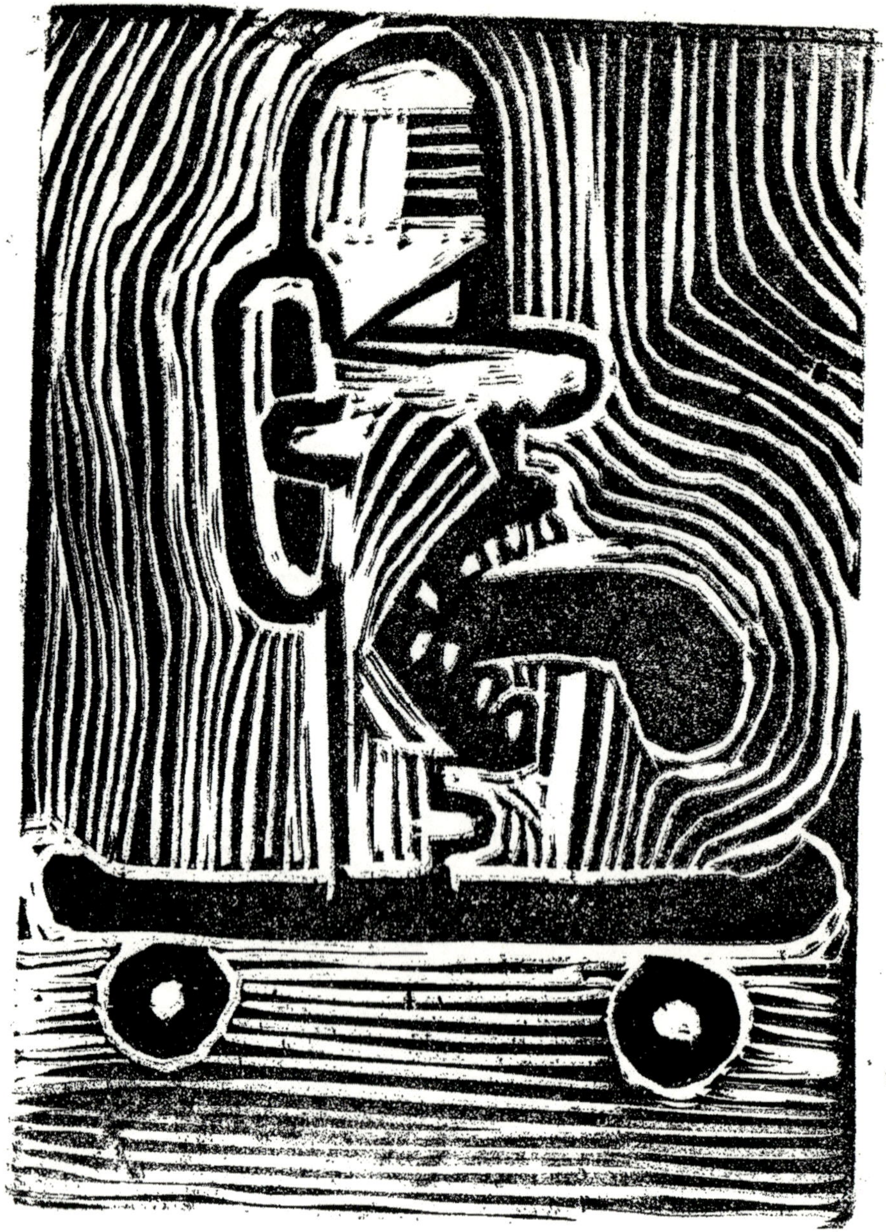

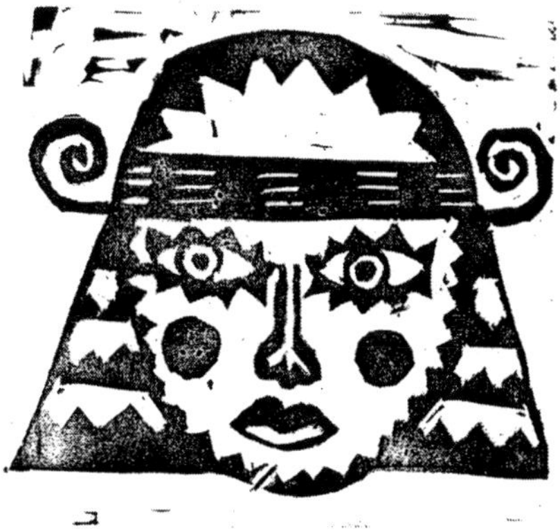

Book 4

Romance

18

A Series of Unfortunate Romances

MY STYLE of asking women out was to get incredibly drunk and then filled with a Dutch courage proceed to blankly ask out anything with the minimum requirement of a vagina and a pulse. Though this was dependant on how drunk I got as I had in the past asked out several men, none of whom had vaginas, a cardboard cut out of woman advertising chopping boards that I met in a Pound Shop and a pile of dirty laundry I had mistaken for a particularly frumpy Goth. This technique had about an 11% success rate and I embarked upon a succession of rather ill fated, short lived and unfortunate romances...

The Beautiful Hippy

THE DRUNK, beautiful hippy girl craned in closer to me surrounded by a musky cloud of nag champa incense and damp unwashed clothes which were no doubt washed in Ecover (which doesn't really work, but no one has the heart to tell them). She started babbling incoherently about how the government had given her too many ballot papers at the last election in a desperate bid to confuse her who to vote for. The drunker she got the more she resembled a boy I went to school with who had a learning

disability, yet somehow she was still highly attractive.
She stormed off in the end when I failed to show enthusiasm for her belief that gluten was a mind controlling agent added to bread by the CIA. I never saw her again.
I went home and consoled myself with a warm glass of ever so slightly gone off milk.

Fat Kelly

I CAUGHT Fat Kelly poking holes in my condoms in the middle of the night.
"I'm desperate for a baby" was her defence

Toni

TONI HAD a strange way of hugging where she would put her arms around your whole body and appear to be squeezing your internal organs like people do with fruit in the supermarket. I awoke one morning in a bath full of ice with a post-it note over a fresh operation scar that just said "Sorry".

Moonpearl

MOONPEARL, she was such a free spirit! So full of life! Though I think her idea of an 'open relationship' had gone a little too far when I came back to find her in bed with the man who worked at the fish counter at our local Sainsbury's Metro, our next door neighbour and what I'm pretty sure was a homeless man.
"There's room at the back somewhere" she said amidst the arms, legs and cocks.

Sue the Muslim

I WAS on my 4th double rum and coke when I realised Sue wasn't drinking. It turns out she was a Muslim and didn't drink. At the end of the evening I was sick a little bit on her hijab and said we should do this again. She informed me that probably wasn't going to happen.

I went home and consoled myself with a warm glass of ever so slightly gone off milk.

Potato Tits

JENNA WAS beautiful, intelligent, creative and kind. The ideal women in all respects. Though unfortunately she had the misfortune of having breasts the exact same size, texture and density of a King Edward potato.

The slightest touch of those cold, hard lumps during lovemaking would extinguish all desire in me.

My mind would instead fixate on potato's and all the foods relating to them...crisps, mash, wedges, Mcain smiley faces, Birds Eye potato waffles etc. until I was so overcome with hunger I would have to get up and get a bag of crisps or go to the local chippy.

We broke up in the end. I'd put on 2 stone.

Posh

I SAW a girl for a while who was a bit on the posh side. It was a real turn on for her to hear about how working class I was. She would go into a frenzy of sexual excitement whenever I mispronounced the names of South American arable crops, referred to a sofa as a 'couch' or my dinner 'tea' or didn't leave wine to breath before drinking it.
One time she caught me making oven chips to dip into some hummus and we made passionate love right there on the cold hard kitchen floor.
   After a while my working class idiosyncrasies started to wear a little thin and I noticed her affections started to wane.
I resorted to making stuff up.
Stories of my old man coming home with a blackened face from 12 hours down the pit, working as a chimney sweep as a child just to help put food on the table.
I even resorted to wearing a flat cap, eating dripping sandwiches and making reactionary, racist and misogynistic statements in a desperate bid to win back her affections.
   Luckily she had been so sheltered from the real world that she didn't know any better. She eventually caught on and broke up with me when she found out I was too young to have have been on the pickets at the Battle of Orgreave as I'd made out.

19

Eyes Like A Feral Animal That Had Accidentally Gotten Drunk On Fermented Apples From Under A Tree

I WAS in the supermarket one day browsing in the reduced section and reached out to grab a discounted vegetable curry slice when my hand inadvertently met with someone else's.

Struck by the beauty of that pale elegant hand I looked up and was confronted with a pair of startling blue eyes, mad and wild like those of a feral animal who had accidentally gotten drunk by eating fermenting apples from under a tree.

We stood clutching the warm slice staring into each others eyes.

Her name was Jem and I managed to gather in our brief conversation that she was an anarcho-nihilist snail farmer who made a living selling her produce to the local 'bourgeois' restaurants. Jem complained a lot about the bourgeois, which meant she was definitely one of them. I explained that I was new to the area and was a writer and artist and invited her to come around for a cup of tea sometime so I could show her my woodcuts.

20
Sexy Medusa

"ARE YOU Ok?" Jem asked in an concerned tone of voice as we sat in my front room awkwardly cradling our cups of tea and looking at my woodcuts.

"Yes, sorry..."

"It's just every time I look at you, you appear to be staring off into the distance..."

If only she knew that I dare not look directly into her eyes, for I feared that if I did so I would melt into a puddle in the presence of such beautific divinity, it was as if she was some kind of ancient demigoddess, like the Medusa, but fitter.

21

Banana Curry

I'D ARRANGED to see Jem again by offering the irresistible temptation of a home made banana curry and a documentary I had got out from the library about moss. There was a little resistance regarding the banana curry which I assured her was a thing...in fact a delicacy in the Kashmir region of India, you know where there make the cardigans.

The combination of too much wine, banana curry and a fascinating documentary about moss was too much to bare and after having declared our undying love for one another we started to tear off each others clothing and made love on the floor as David Attenborough announced that was moss was over 252.2 million years old and can be found in fossils dating back to the Permian period.

22

Marvel Pants

As SHE slid down her skirt it revealed her glorious ass in a pair of Marvel underpants. The muscular green Hulk and the web slinging Spider-Man displayed boldly on either side of her perfect round cheeks.
It was then that I knew I would love her forever.
Upstairs she lay naked on the bed, her beautiful face and body illuminated by the glow of the Pound Land LED fairy lights that were entwined around the head of the bed.
On her lips lay the most radiant and contented of smiles.
I couldn't think of anything more beautiful that I'd ever seen.
I sat and treasured this moment, hoping that it would last forever and stay engraved onto my memory until the day I died.
But I knew it was only a matter of time before this moment would be taken away from me and the vision of this beautiful goddess would be gone, lost once more to the darkness...
As I'd also gotten the batteries that powered the lights from the pound shop and everyone knew they didn't last very long.

23

Husband In A Coma

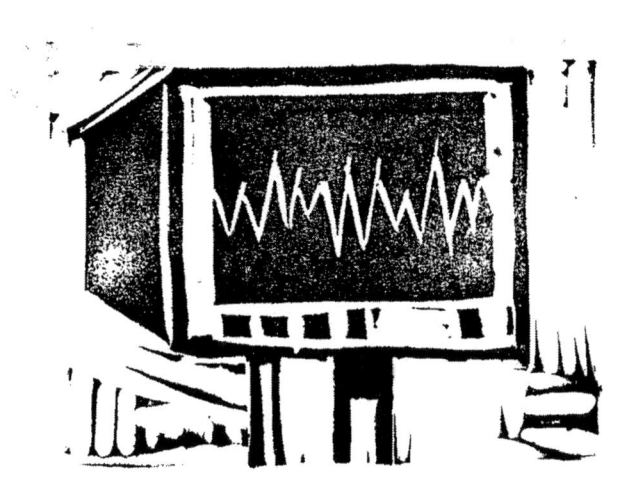

"I'M SORT of married" Jem confessed the next morning
A strange "Ahhh" like noise emanated from my mouth for several minutes followed by several minutes' silence.
"Like as in proper married-married or separated soon to be divorced? I asked
"Proper married...only, my husband is in a sort-of-coma"
"As in a real coma-coma or an emotional-coma? Like he doesn't listen to your needs and stuff and is generally very cold and distant? Like he never asks you how your day went. That sort of thing"
"Oh nothing serious and complex like that, just a regular coma with the tubes and machine that goes ping and all that."

"What happened?"
"He was hit by a milk float one day on his way to work. The doctors said if the float had been carrying an extra two pints it would have killed him. I just thank god for the decline in the milk delivering industry"

"I'd been intending on divorcing him pre-coma but just felt it would be a bit insensitive divorcing someone in that state. Also I want to see the crushed look of despair in his eyes when I tell him I'm leaving him"
So here she was in relationship limbo.

24

Pound Shop Viagra

REGARDLESS OF the fidelity grey area for the next fortnight our genitals were inseparable. It had been some time for Jem and to meet the voracious sexual demands of my new lover I'd started to take Pound shop Viagra.

Though I stopped taking this when my semen started to come out blue.

25

Thrush

ONE MORNING I awoke to the smell of freshly baked bread which was rather pleasant until I realised it was coming from my genitals.

"Hi, I would like to speak to someone about getting checked over, I've been having unprotected intercourse with a sort-of-married women" I told the lady at the sexual health clinic
"OK sir, please fill in this form, and take one of our loyalty cards..."
"Loyalty cards? Oh sorry I won't be needing one of those. I'm really not that sort of person"

"That's what they all say..." she said nodding towards the waiting room full of pale, anxious, STD victims who were all fidgeting in their seats and clutching bags of frozen peas to their genitals.
"On your sixth visit you get a complimentary dildo" she said encouragingly brandishing a large dildo with "Safe Sex" printed on its wobbling side.

It turns out I had thrush and needed some cream to treat it but was disgusted to realise it was now £8.70 for a prescription. This, added to the fact that I was now banned from all the chemists in the city for a minor abuse of over the counter cold and flu remedies meant I had no way of getting it.
I looked it up and apparently you could get the same effect by submerging the infected area into natural yogurt.
Which I also didn't have.
I did have loads of ever so slightly gone off milk though.
And milks pretty much the same thing as yogurt isn't it? I reasoned.

26

A Series of Unfortunate Coffees

JEM SLOWLY initiated me into the rites of the middle-classes. The most sacred of all these was 'Going for a coffee' where every 5 minutes you were expected to drink over priced pseudo-gourmet coffee in one of the cities never ending supply of gimmicky, fad coffee shops...

I.V's

I sat in an uncomfortable green plastic chair as a large double latte slowly entered my blood stream via an intravenous drip.
Jem sat opposite having a macchiato enema while reading a magazine.

The Cobblers

The waiter placed a large soggy boot full of coffee onto the table as Jem delicately sipped her double espresso from a red stiletto.

Junkies

"I love this place" Jem said as she injected a shot of double espresso into her main line.
"Do you know everything is served in recycled needles?"
"Yeah it's great" I said looking dubiously at my syringe full of steaming latte
"Is it possible to get mine in a mug though?" I asked

Essence of Coffee

In the Essence Of Coffee you were seated and were allowed to smell a variety of jars of coffee...
"I bet that would taste really good" Jem said
"Yeah it's a shame we can't have one"
Jem tutted and rolled her eyes.

27

Yarpool

FOR THE last few months Jem had been asking to go to the infamous town of my birth. She'd heard rumours and gossip of incest, cannibalism and ham skidding and was intrigued. I finally caved in and agreed to go there on a day trip.

"Have you had your immunisation jabs recently? And remember don't go near the seagulls they have herpes...also don't drink the water, I took a girl here once and she still hasn't got rid of her diarrhoea. And that was 4 years ago" I manically instructed Jem as we boarded the bright yellow bus.

We got off at the bus station and headed for one of the towns plethora of chip stalls.

In the que Jems eyes scanned the condiments on display...

"4 types of vinegar, wow!" Jem exclaimed at the vast variety of vinegar on offer.

"I wonder if they have balsamic..."

There was a stunned silence as the whole market place turned towards us...

"I'm sorry she didn't know!" I implored to the gathering mass
We were chased from market place by an angry mob brandishing razor sharp potato peelers and gone off pickled eggs.

28

The Old Man and the Pigeons

WE TOOK refuge in my old man's place. He ran a shop close to the town centre.
Although calling it a shop is a very liberal use of the word.
It sold a eclectic range of miscellania and detritus...mouldy country and western records, 70's sci-fi paperbacks, rusty tools, a pigs skull with a machete embedded into its cranium, a burnt doll that was nailed to the ceiling and charm bracelets.

Though it was hard to discern what was on offer on account of the fine layer of crusty white bird shit and feathers that covered everything. This was the produce of the the dozens of pigeons that also inhabited the place.
Though these weren't for sale.
They occupied every available nook and crevice including my old man's cardigan pockets.
He had taken a rather liberal approach to their nesting a few years ago and now he was over run. Though they added to the shops general turmoil which pleased him greatly.
It had never been my old mans dream to run a shop and it perplexed both himself and his customers why he did so. Though they had a mutual understanding: He didn't want them in there and they had often regretted coming in.
It was his dream to make the place so inhospitable that he would never have a customer again and could finally have some peace and quiet.
I took one look around the place and suggested we go to the pub.

29

Spyder, Voldak and Terry

IN THE pub we were met by its resident alcoholics Spyder, Voldak and Terry. The landlord used to joke that between them they'd help to pay off his mortage. Which was probably true.

Spyder

They called him Spyder as he was tall, spindley and always dressed in black. He also had a massive tattoo of a spider displayed prominently in the centre of his forehead.

Voldak

In his own country he was a famous bear* wrestler. His thick beard and hair were covered in scars like pink roads cut into in a dark forest.

Terry

He hadn't worn a shirt since 1969 and his skin now resembled a pork scratching that had been left under a sun bed

"I'll tell you one thing about Thatcher..." said my old man after his 3rd pint
"Sorry dad we have to go..." I announced sensing a storm brewing inside the old man's head which would inevitably end in violence or the Luddistic smashing of technology.
Before we left the old man opened his enormous hands to reveal two tiny white eggs.

*I later learnt this was not the animal but the category of homosexual. Apparently wrestling gay, overweight, hairy men is a highly respected cultural pastime in Eastern Europe.

30

Bus

SHE LAY sleeping on the bus against the window silhouetted against the miles and miles of flat landscape that stretched towards the horizon behind her.
She looked beautiful. Like a marble white Grecian statue.
While she slept I gently inspected her clothing and hair for any lice or fleas she may have picked up.

31

Break

"Iᴛ's MY husband...he's awake!" Jem announced one morning on the phone

"Oh great!" I said feigning enthusiasm with all my soul while my heart slowly shattered to a thousand pieces inside my chest.

There was an awkward pause.

"So...what happens to us?" I asked

"I...need some time to think. Maybe we should have a break for a bit?"

I put down the phone and pulled up a chair next to my weeping cousin who gave me an acknowledging nod and pushed the bottle of whiskey towards me.

32

Without You

WITHOUT JEM I felt that a part of me was missing.
Quite a large part too.
Like a nipple of an elbow.

33

Untitled

"IT'S MY husband, he's been hit by another milk float and is in another coma" Jem announced on the phone a few days later
"Oh no, that's terrible" I said concealing my delight with every ounce of my being.
"It was the same driver...the doctors said it was a one in a million chance. Luckily he's been put on a 6 month driving ban"
"It sounds like you could really do with a hug"
"Yes, I really could. I know I've messed you about but do you think you could come over?"
"Yeah sure," I said nonchalantly

"There's a few things I've got on at the moment but nothing I couldn't move around" I lied
"See you in a bit" I put down the phone and skipped all the way over to her place.

34

Little People That Came Out Of My Vagina

"I SORT of have children" Jem announced one morning
"Sort of...as in?"
"As in little people that came out of my vagina"
"I have a little boy and girl. Maybe you should meet them."

35

My Special Friend

WE STOOD in front of the two children who eyed me up and down suspiciously.
"I'd like to introduce you to my *special friend...*" she said
They weren't buying it.
I opened my mouth to speak
"You're not my real dad!" the boy screamed running to his room and slamming the door behind him.
The little girl eyed me up and down stoney eyed before turning and walking silently out of the room.

36

Mashed Potato

"CAN YOU come over? Something's happened..." Jem hurriedly told me on the phone.
I ran over to her place anxious about what it could be. Was her husband out of his 2nd coma? I weighed up how I would feel about Jem declaring that she was a man, had excessive library fines or was a video pirate.

When I got there Jem and the children were circled around a hot water bottle on top of a sardine tin in the back garden. Jem removed it to reveal the two tiny white eggs which were moving and starting to crack.

We all huddled around and stared in silent wonder as the eggs slowly cracked opened revealing two scrawny grey birds. There black eyes slowly opened as the gazed out onto their new world. They let out a tiny chirp.

"They look hungry…what shall we feed them?" Asked the little girl looking up to me

"Mashed potato?" I shrugged.

Epilogue

"SO, WHAT happened to that book you were writing?" Jem asked one day
"Oh yeah, I've probably got enough material for it by now. Though it would be good to have one more big thing to put in it, like for dramatic closure or something. A cliff-hanger as such. Something to tie together the other stuff, something big so people would forget that the other stuff wasn't very good and I only wrote the whole thing because I had loads of ISBN numbers to use up."
"Well..." said my beautiful girlfriend inhaling deeply in anxious anticipation.
"I'm pregnant"

*37

The Bedsit Chapter

THE ESTATE agent showed me around the contents of the grotty, damp bedsit.
"Jesus" I thought to myself "so this is it."
"So, what do you think? £440 per calender month, we could get all the paper work done today and you could be in by Monday."
"Oh no sorry, I have no interest in renting it, its for research really"
"Oh..." said the estate agent, clearly annoyed.
"Research for what? A film?" he said his annoyance giving way to curiosity
"Oh no it's for a book"
"Oh really, what's the book about?"
"It's about a man who doesn't live in a bedsit"

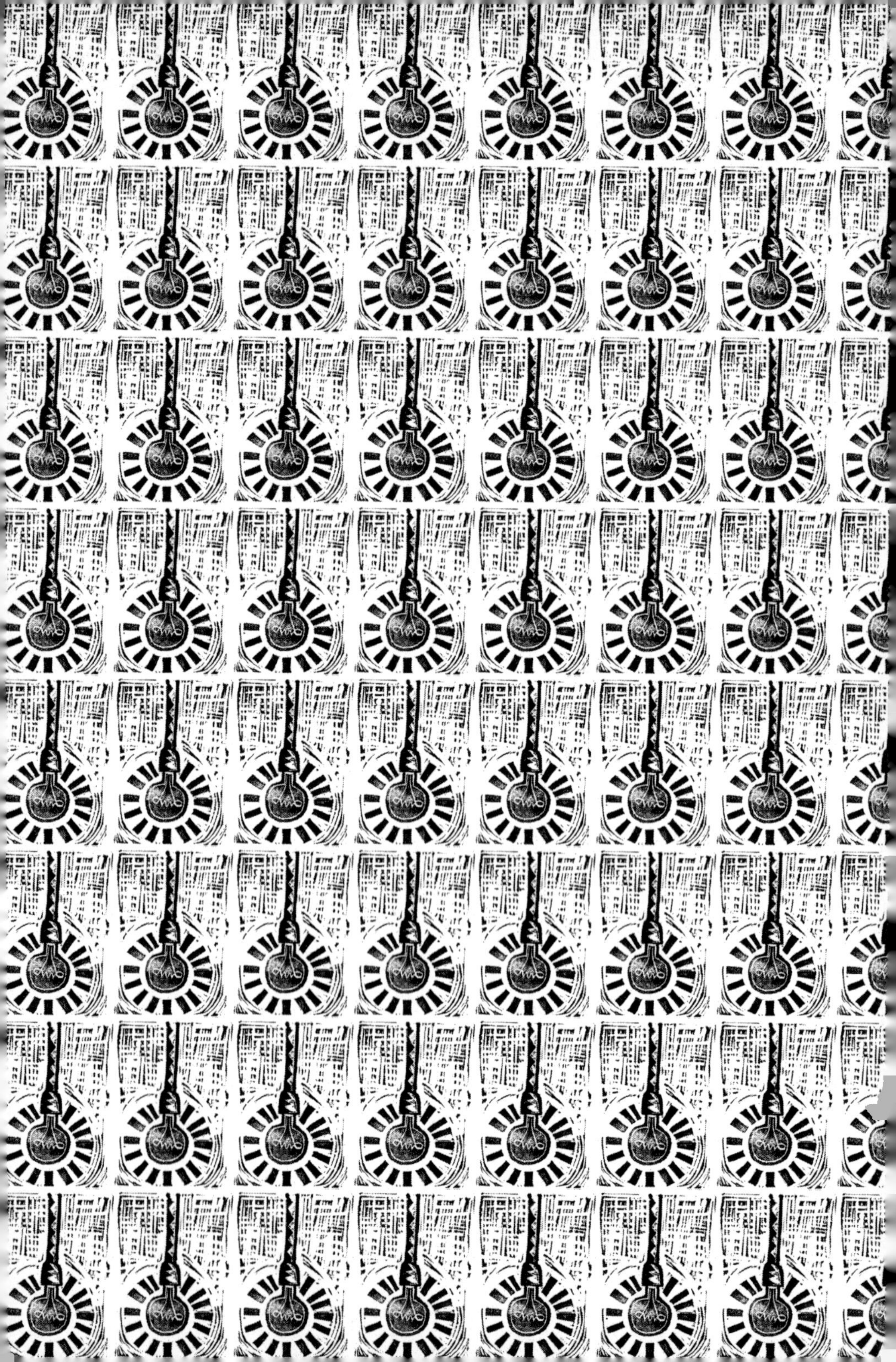